Flabbersmashed About You

by Rachel Vail • illustrated by Yumi Heo

Feiwel and Friends   New York

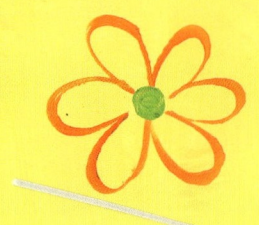

A FEIWEL AND FRIENDS BOOK
An Imprint of Macmillan

FLABBERSMASHED ABOUT YOU. Text copyright © 2012 by Rachel Vail.
Illustrations copyright © 2012 by Yumi Heo. All rights reserved.
Printed in China by South China
Printing Co. Ltd., Dongguan City, Guangdong Province.
For information, address Feiwel and Friends,
175 Fifth Avenue, New York, N.Y. 10010.

Library of Congress Cataloging-in-Publication Data

Vail, Rachel.
Flabbersmashed about you / by Rachel Vail ;
illustrated by Yumi Heo. — 1st ed.
p. cm.
Summary: When Katie's best friend Jennifer plays with Roy
at recess instead of with her, Katie is surprised and angry.
ISBN: 978-0-312-61345-7
[1. Best friends—Fiction. 2. Friendship—Fiction.
3. Schools—Fiction.] I. Heo, Yumi, ill. II. Title.
PZ7.V1916Fl 2012 [E]—dc22 2011004079

Feiwel and Friends logo designed by Filomena Tuosto

First Edition: 2012
The artwork was created with oil and pencil on
Fabriano watercolor paper coated with gesso.

1 3 5 7 9 10 8 6 4 2

mackids.com

To Mom, my first and forever friend —R.V.

For best friends Pepper, Parker, and General James —Y.H.

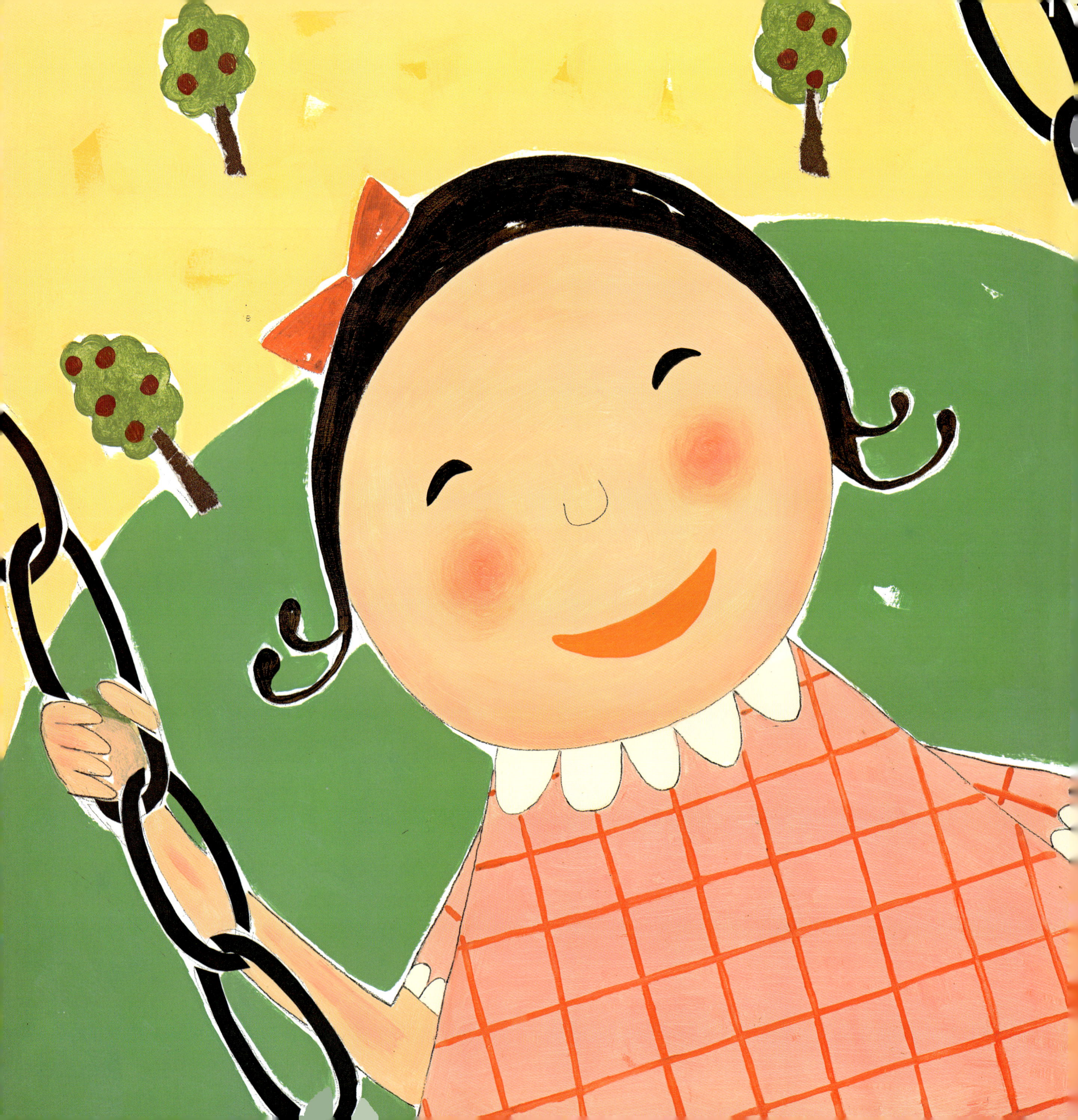

My name is

Katie Honors,

and I'm a really friendly kid.

I like to play with everybody, and they all like to play with me, too.

I go on lots of playdates.

My whole class gets invited to

MY BIRTHDAY PARTY.

Even Arabella, who just moved here and hardly talks at all.

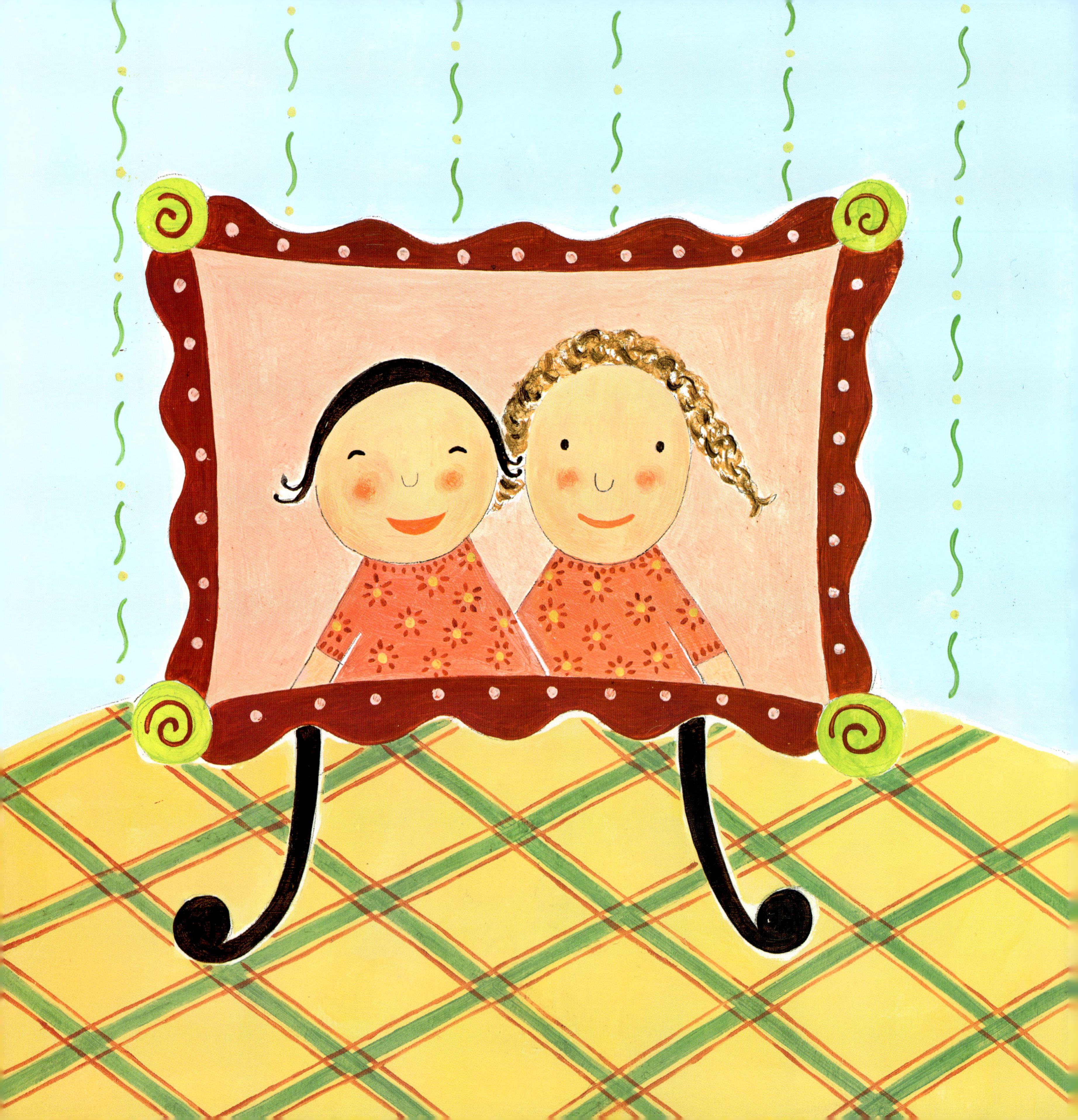

My **best friend** in the whole entire world is JENNIFER.

We have been best friends **forever**.

Her smile is as bright as the morning sun in your eyes.

Lots of times, we dress alike. Our hands fit **perfectly** together.

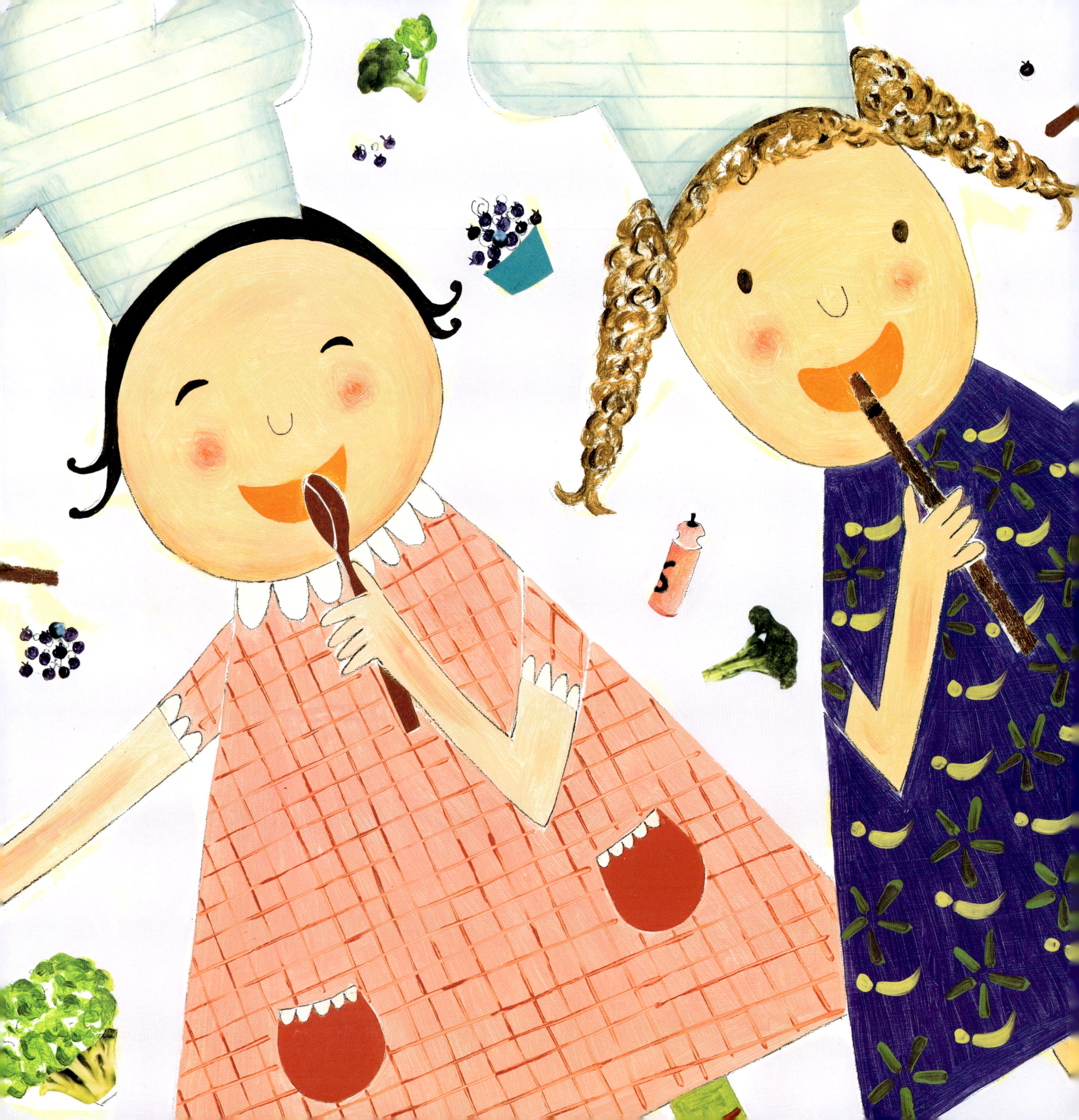
S

We cook imaginary broccoli-blueberry soup and put on shows together.
I say, **"Ladies and Gentlemen!"** and Jennifer says, **"And children of all ages!"**
We use sticks as our microphones, and also as our soup ladles.
We always choose each other as walk-in-from-recess buddies.

UNTIL TODAY.

Today at recess, Jennifer did not want to make soup or put on a show. She wanted to play warriors with Roy and kill the bad guys.

I don't like killing bad guys.

I like soup. And shows.

I told Jennifer she could be the one saying "Ladies and Gentlemen!" but she was too busy building a fort and laughing.

WITH ROY.

The playground felt very

HUGE.

I stood all alone in the
middle of it, completely

Flabbersmashed.

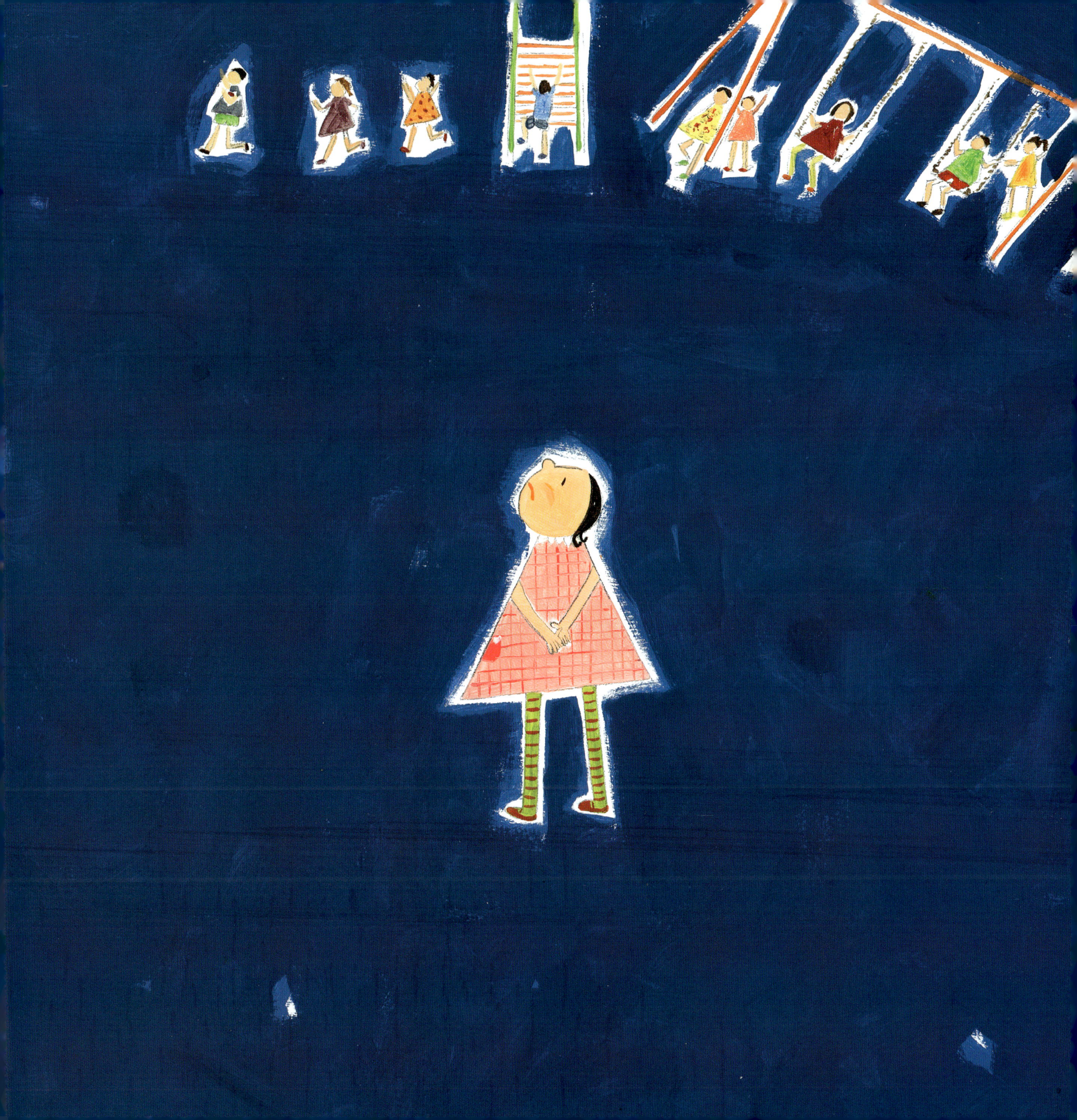

My best friend Jennifer and that kid Roy
ran right past me,
chasing imaginary bad guys together.
They didn't bump into me, but still,

my whole self felt like a bruise.

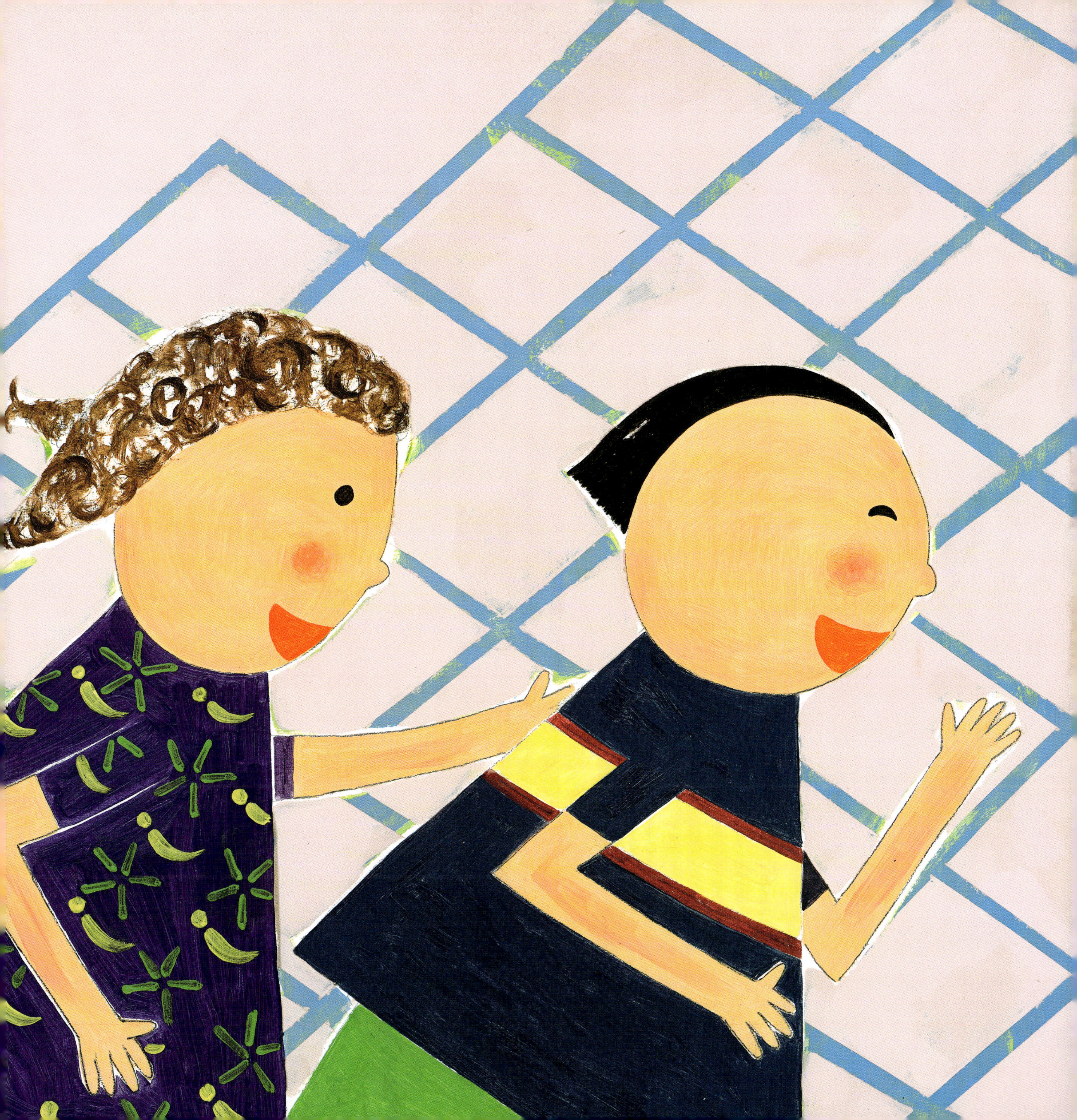

I thought of sixty-seven million mean things to yell at Jennifer.

And a gagillion bajillion quadrillion

even meaner things to yell at that AWFUL Roy.

But if I opened my mouth to **yell** any of those mean things, what might have come out was **crying**.

So, I kept my mouth closed.

When it was time to line up to go in after recess, Jennifer chose **Roy** to be her buddy.

I chopped their hands apart and said, "No leaving me out!"

"We're not," Jennifer said, "but you can only choose one walk-in-from-recess buddy at a time."

She held hands with Roy again, and they walked inside together.

I yelled at Jennifer's back,

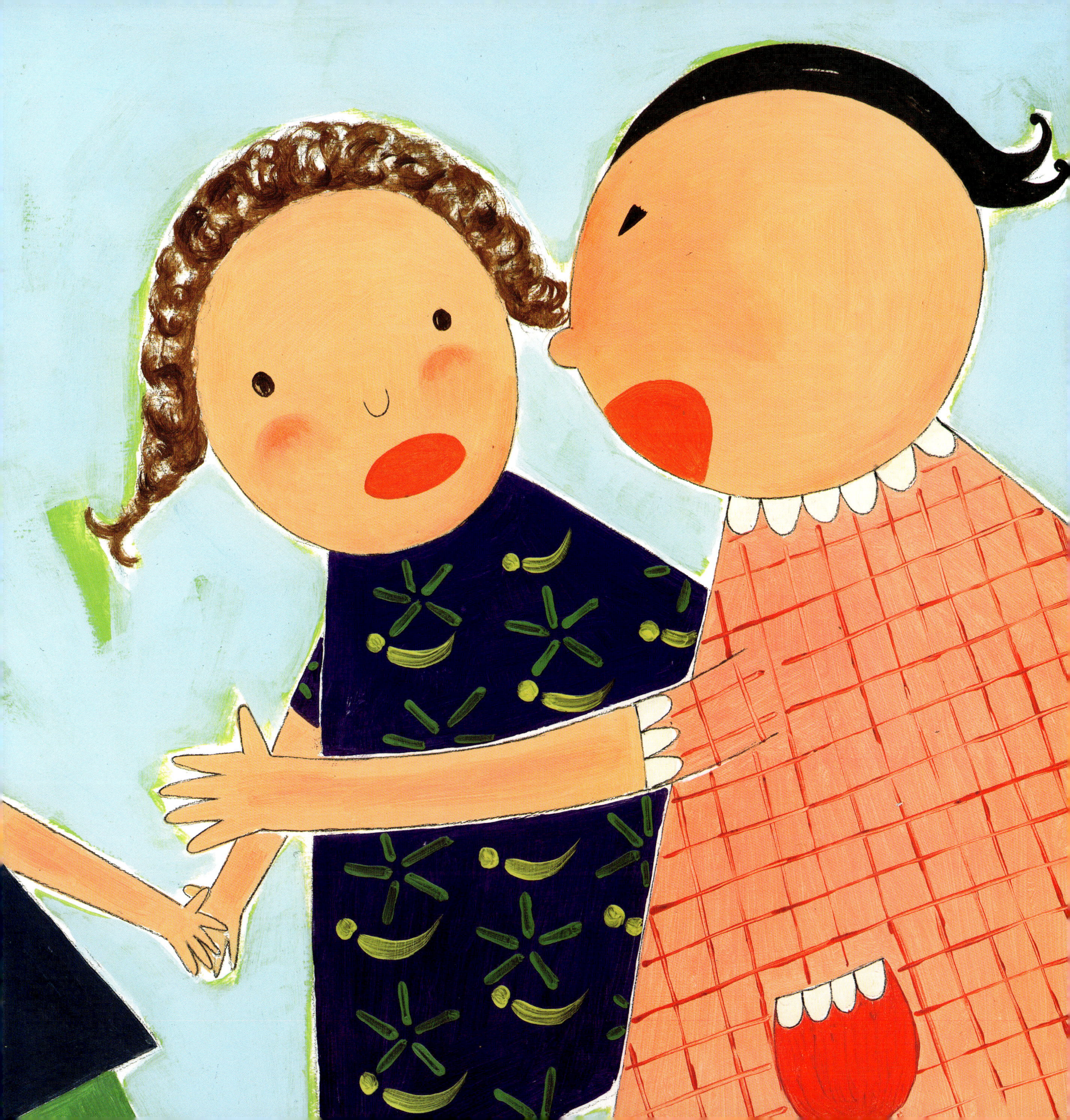

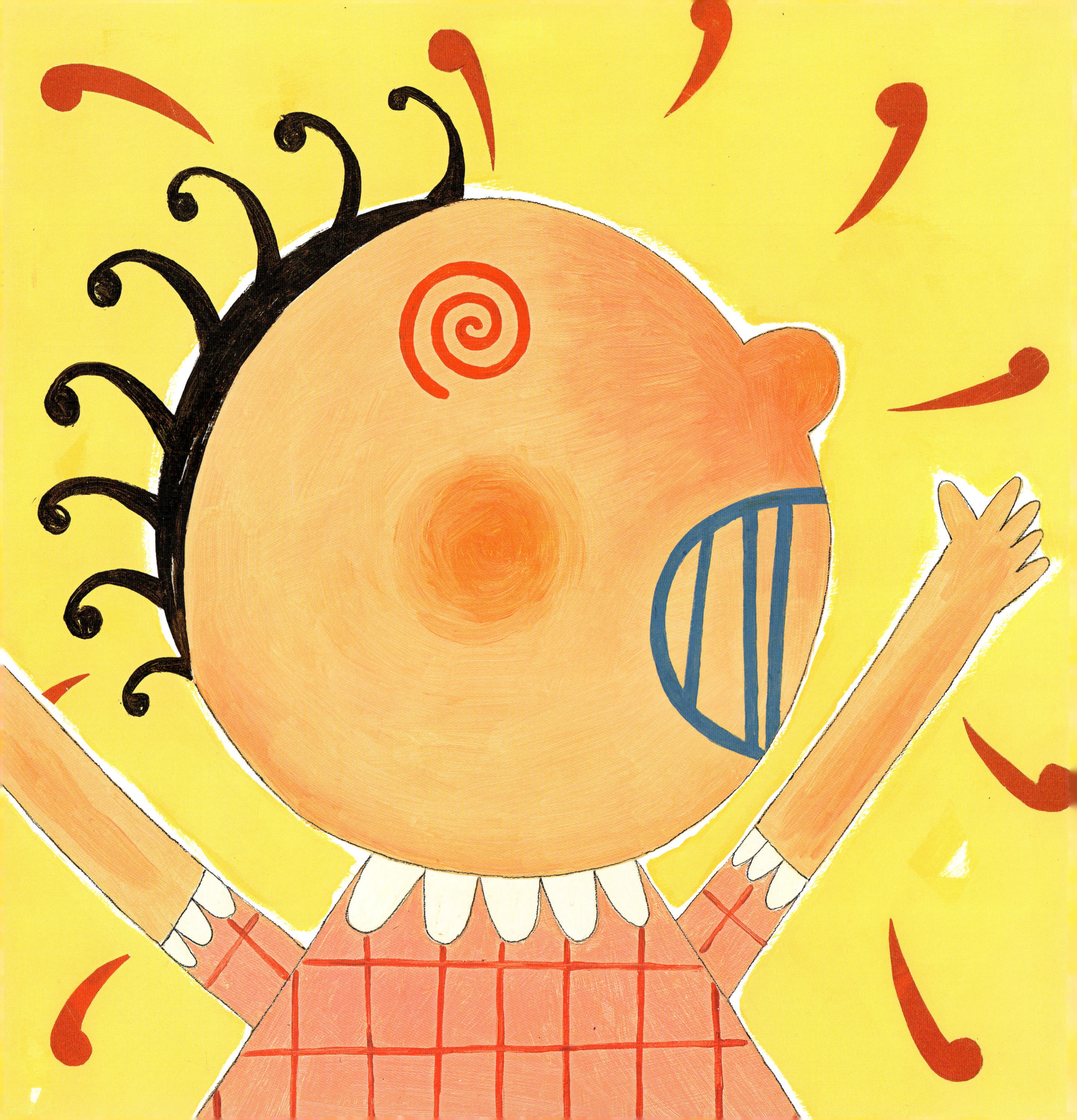

"I am Flabbersmashed about YOU!"

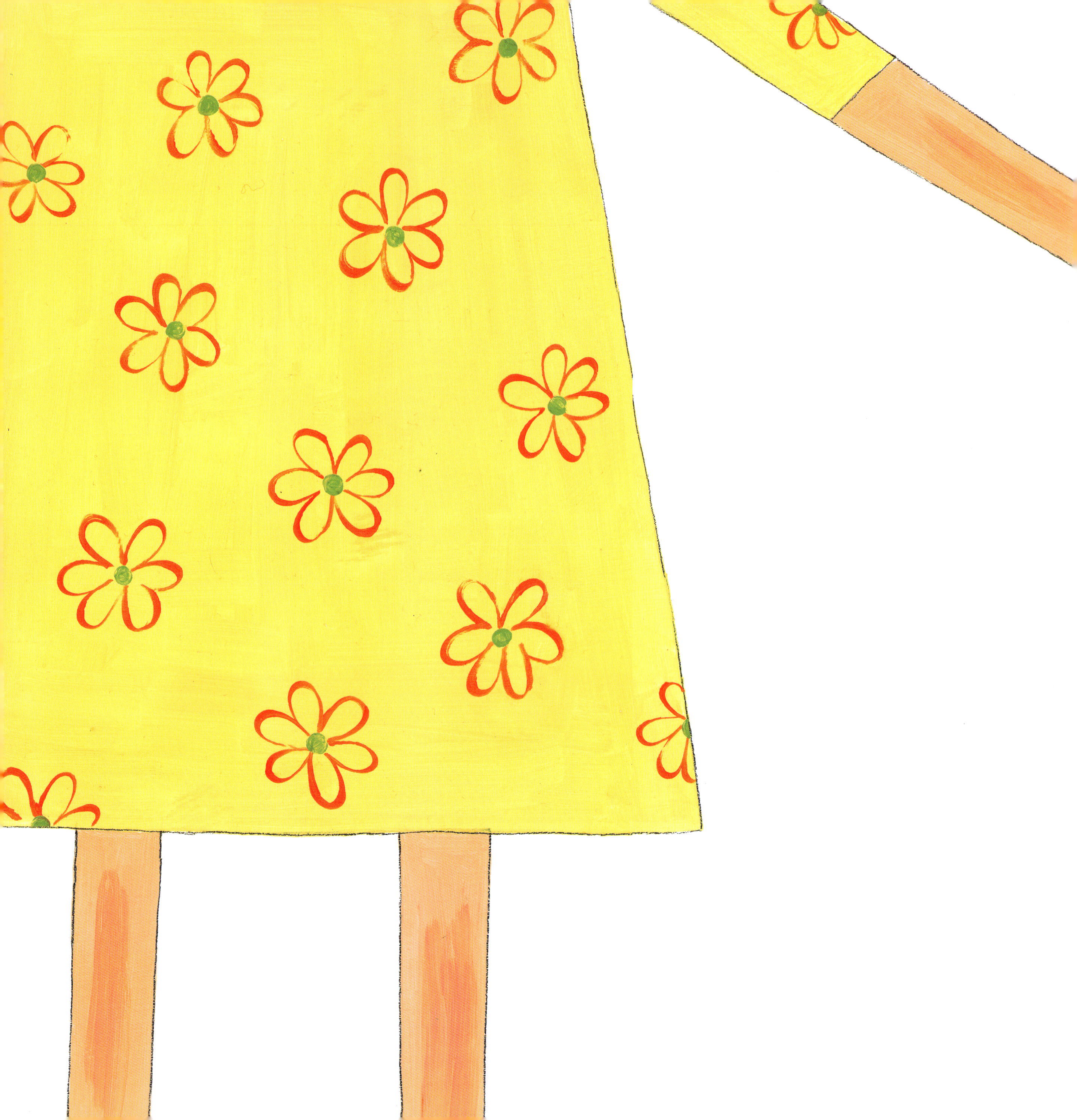

Somebody's hand slipped into mine. It was **Arabella's.** Her hand was smaller than Jennifer's.

I sniffed and said, "Jennifer is my best friend."
"I know," Arabella whispered.

Arabella's hand **was not** JENNIFER'S hand.

But it fit okay with mine, too.

"Do you like making pretend soup?" I asked her.

"I don't know," Arabella said.

"It sounds like FUN."

I took a big breath and asked,

"More fun than killing bad guys?"

Arabella nodded, and then she smiled. Her smile was gentle like the afternoon sun between the leaves.

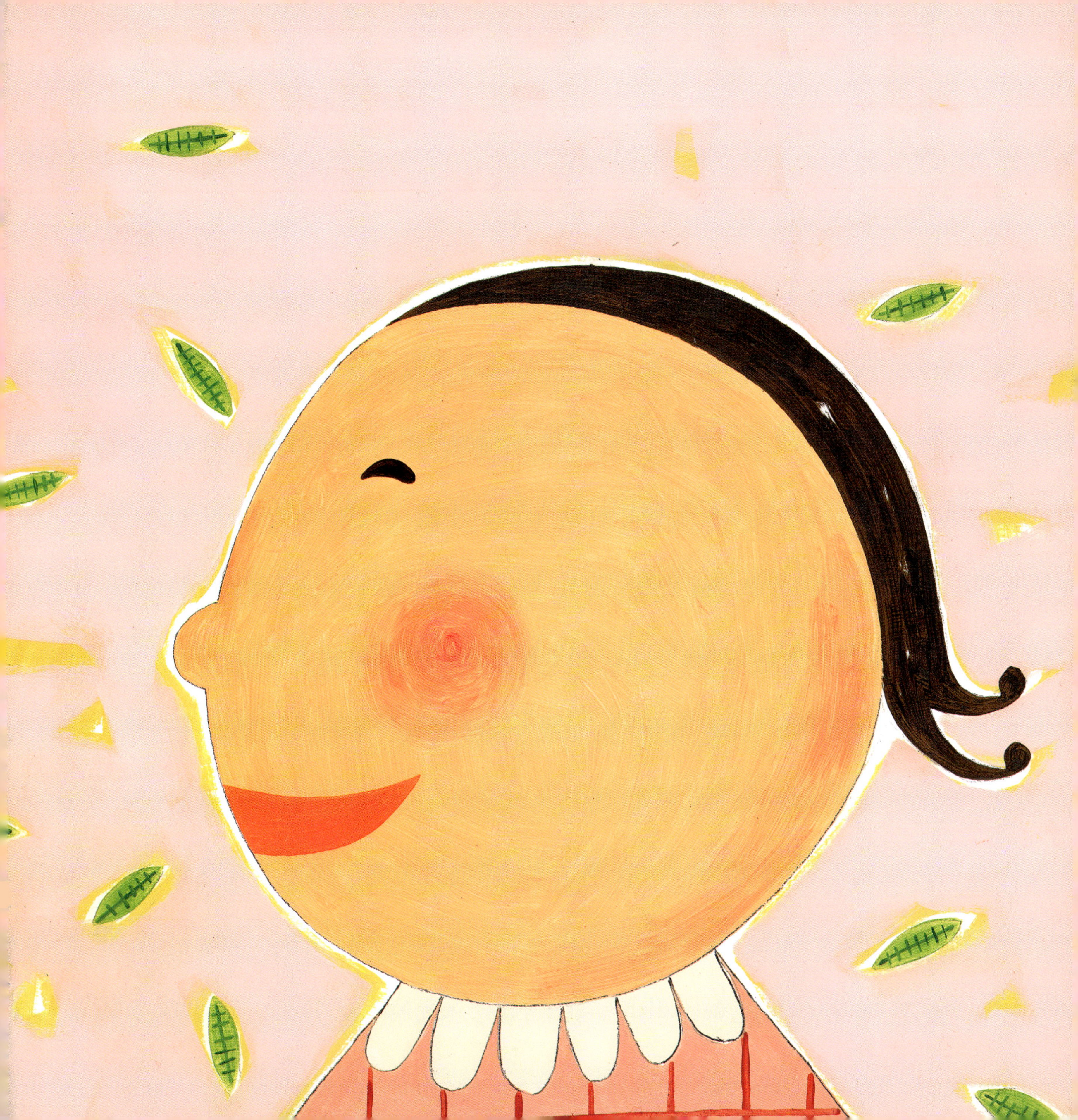

I gave her hand
a little squeeze
and then
we walked inside
TOGETHER.